Nothing But Trouble

COME ON...YOU DON'T *REALLY* WANT TO READ THIS BOOK, DO YOU? I MEAN, I'M SURE IT'S VERY INACCURATE. IT'S PROBABLY FULL OF LIES AND STORIES ABOUT HOW I CAN NEVER DO ANYTHING RIGHT AND THAT ALL MY PLANS ARE SO SILLY AND...AND...

ADAPTED BY JOHN GREEN

BASED ON THE SERIES CREATED BY
DAN POVENMIRE & JEFF "SWAMPY" MARSH

DISNEY PRESS

NEW YORK

LIBRARY OF CONGRESS CATALOG CARD NUMBER ON FILE.
ISBN 978-1-4231-4055-9
FIRST EDITION
1 3 5 7 9 10 8 6 4 2
PRINTED IN THE UNITED STATES OF AMERICA
G658-7729-4-10152

FOR MORE DISNEY PRESS FUN, VISIT WWW.DISNEYBOOKS.COM
VISIT DISNEYCHANNEL.COM

SUMMER VACATION! THERE'S A WHOLE LOT OF STUFF TO DO BEFORE SCHOOL STARTS, AND *PHINEAS AND FERB* PLAN TO DO IT ALL! MAYBE THEY'LL BUILD A ROCKET, OR FIND FRANKENSTEIN'S BRAIN...WHATEVER THEY DO, THEY'RE SURE TO ANNOY THEIR SISTER, *CANDACE*. MEANWHILE, THEIR FAMILY PET, *PERRY* THE PLATYPUS, LEADS A DOUBLE LIFE AS AGENT P, FACING OFF AGAINST THE DEVIOUS *DR. DOOFENSHMIRTZ!*

"DAY OF THE LIVING GELATIN!"

AS PRESIDENT OF THE HEALTHY DESSERT CLUB--

--I DECLARE THAT NOTHING SAYS "LOW CALORIE, NONFAT" MORE THAN GELATIN.

YOU WOULDN'T HAVE STARTED THIS CLUB BECAUSE GELATIN IS JEREMY'S FAVORITE DESSERT, WOULD YOU?

WHAT? N-NO.

EW, *GROSS.*

PHINEAS AND FERB! YOUR SMELLY RODENT-PET IS GERMING UP THE CABINETS.

WHERE *ARE* THOSE TWO?

RIGHT HERE, CANDACE.

BUT HOW--HOW DID YOU GET THERE--WHERE YOU ARE--SO FAST?!?

OH, WE WERE JUST PUTTING THE FINISHING TOUCHES ON OUR MOLECULAR TRANSPORTER. WOULD YOU LIKE TO TRY?

DO I *LOOK* LIKE SOMEONE WHO WANTS THEIR MOLECULES TRANSPORTED?

NOW, GET THAT STINKY PET OUT OF OUR CABINETS AND GO SCRAMBLE YOUR MOLECULES SOMEWHERE ELSE.

WOULD YOU GUYS LIKE TO TRY SOME OF OUR GELATIN?

NO, WAIT. THEY'LL JUST END UP DOING SOMETHING WEIRD AND RUIN THE PARTY.

HOW IS SHARING GELATIN WITH THEM GONNA RUIN THE PARTY?

SOME...
...HOW?

YOU WANT CHERRY OR GRAPE?

GRAPE, PLEASE!

IT'S AS FUN TO EAT AS THE CRAZY, FUN THINGS YOU CAN DO WITH IT!

SPROING!

WOBBLE!

BOUNCE!

THE CARTILAGINOUS FIBERS FROM THE BOVINE PATELLA STRUCTURE THAT GELATIN'S EXTRACTED FROM GIVES IT THAT FUN, BOUNCY QUALITY.

WHAT DID I TELL YOU? WEIRD. NOW, LET THE PROFESSIONAL HANDLE THIS BEFORE IT GETS OUTTA HAND.

WHY DON'T YOU MAKE YOUR *OWN* GELATIN AND LEAVE US ALONE.

FERB, I KNOW WHAT WE'RE GONNA DO TODAY.

BYE, CANDACE.

WAIT! I'M NOT FINISHED! STAY AWAY FROM ME AND MY FRIENDS AND MY GELATIN THAT I DON'T WANT *RUINED* WITH YOUR *RUINY RUINNESS.* HMPH!!

WHAT?

SOON...

HEY, ISABELLA. THANKS FOR LETTING US USE YOUR SWIMMING POOL AS THE LARGEST GELATIN MOLD EVER.

YOU BET.

FERB, RELEASE THE GELATIN MIX.

RRRUMBLE

GELATIN

RELEASE!

OOH, OOH, OOH! MAY I ADD SOME OF *MY* FAVORITE FLAVOR?

SURE, BUDDY.

HEE-HEE-HEE!

STIRRING TEAM, COMMENCE MIXING OPERATIONS.

AYE-AYE.

HEY, WHERE'S PERRY?

GOOD QUESTION, PHINEAS! WHERE *IS* PERRY?!?

GRAB!

WHOOOSH!

AH, THERE YOU ARE, AGENT P.

DOOFENSHMIRTZ HAS SENT YOU A VIDEO MESSAGE. TAKE A LOOK.

OH, HELLO, PERRY THE PLATYPUS! I'M SURE YOU'RE GETTING THIS. I-I WAS *HOPING* YOU WOULD STOP BY TODAY FOR SOME *TEA.*

SEE, I'VE GOT ALL THESE LITTLE *TEA THINGS* SET OUT AND READY, AND, UM...

AND, P-PLEASE USE THE *FRONT ENTRANCE,* PERRY THE PLATYPUS, BECAUSE, UH...

...BECAUSE ALL THE OTHER ENTRANCES DON'T WORK TODAY. SO BYE-BYE. I'LL SEE YOU LATER TODAY.

COMING IN THROUGH THE FRONT ENTRANCE.

SO YOU SEE, DOOFENSHMIRTZ HAS INVITED YOU TO TEA. WE DON'T KNOW WHAT IT COULD POSSIBLY MEAN.

WE THINK--BUT DON'T HOLD US TO THIS-- WE THINK THAT MAYBE, *JUST MAYBE,* IT COULD BE A TRAP.

WE DO, HOWEVER, LIKE TO GIVE PEOPLE THE BENEFIT OF THE DOUBT, SO TRY TO HAVE FUN. *MONOGRAM OUT.*

AS PERRY RACES OFF FOR TEA...

HOW'S IT LOOKIN', PHINEAS?

LOOKS GOOD. AND JUDGING BY MY CHRONOMETER, IT SHOULD BE JUST ABOUT TIME. THERE'S ONLY ONE THING TO DO NOW.

YOU MEAN TEST THE RESILIENCY OF OUR CARTILAGINOUS COLLUSION WITH VIGOROUS APPLICATION OF WEIGHT AND VELOCITY?

EXACTLY. LET'S JUMP ON IT!

BWONG!

WHEE!

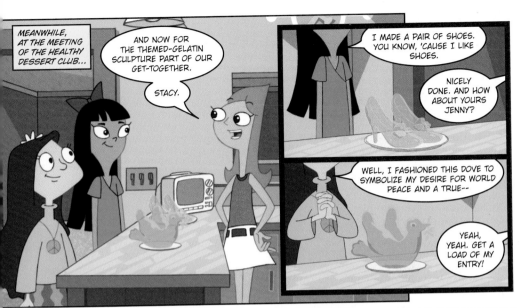

MEANWHILE, AT THE MEETING OF THE HEALTHY DESSERT CLUB...

AND NOW FOR THE THEMED-GELATIN SCULPTURE PART OF OUR GET-TOGETHER.

STACY.

I MADE A PAIR OF SHOES. YOU KNOW, 'CAUSE I LIKE SHOES.

NICELY DONE. AND HOW ABOUT YOURS JENNY?

WELL, I FASHIONED THIS DOVE TO SYMBOLIZE MY DESIRE FOR WORLD PEACE AND A TRUE--

YEAH, YEAH. GET A LOAD OF MY ENTRY!

IT'S JEREMY'S HEAD!

WATCH, I CAN EVEN MAKE HIM DANCE--

WHEE!

HEY, WHAT'S THAT?

SOUNDS LIKE FUN.

WHAT?

BWONG!

THAT LOOKS AWESOME.

WE SHOULD GO OVER THERE AND CHECK IT OUT.

TOTALLY.

BWONG!

BUT THAT'S JUST PHINEAS AND FERB AND THEIR FRIENDS.

DON'T BE SO UPTIGHT.

YEAH, COME ON.

NAH, IT'S OKAY. GO AHEAD.

BWONG!

THAT DOES LOOK KINDA FUN.

MAYBE I SHOULD...

...TOTALLY BUST THEM FOR THIS!!

MEANWHILE...

Doofenshmirtz Evil Inc.

THIS IS NICE, HUH?

YOU KNOW, I WAS THINKING THE OTHER DAY ABOUT HOW MUCH BETTER YOU WOULD BE AS AN *ALLY*.

SO I-- CREATED *THIS*!

beep!

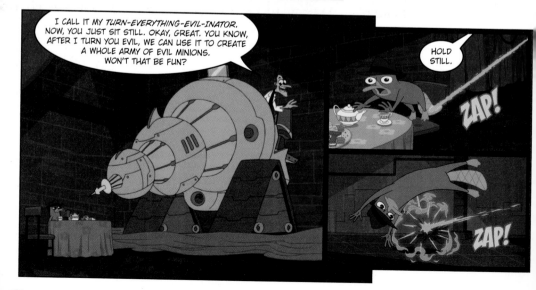

I CALL IT MY *TURN-EVERYTHING-EVIL-INATOR*. NOW, YOU JUST SIT STILL. OKAY, GREAT. YOU KNOW, AFTER I TURN YOU EVIL, WE CAN USE IT TO CREATE A WHOLE ARMY OF EVIL MINIONS. WON'T THAT BE FUN?

HOLD STILL.

ZAP!

ZAP!

WHAT THE--?

WAIT TILL MOM SEES *THIS!*

GRAAR!

gulp!

BUT HOW DO WE FIGHT A GELATIN MONSTER?

WE'LL BEAT HIM THE SAME WAY WE CREATED HIM-- WITH *WATER.*

YOU GUYS ARE SO BUSTED!

WELL, I GUESS WE'D BETTER RESCUE CANDACE.

AND THIS ROPE MIGHT COME IN HANDY, TOO.

TO THE MUNITIONS DEPOT!

GRAAR!

YOU'RE JUST MAKING HIM ANGRY!

SPLAT!

HE'S CHARGING! GET READY!

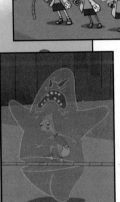

EVERYBODY. PULL!

splorp!

WAAA!

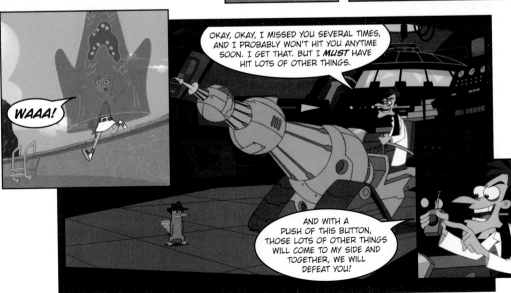

OKAY, OKAY, I MISSED YOU SEVERAL TIMES, AND I PROBABLY WON'T HIT YOU ANYTIME SOON. I GET THAT. BUT I *MUST* HAVE HIT LOTS OF OTHER THINGS.

AND WITH A PUSH OF THIS BUTTON, THOSE LOTS OF OTHER THINGS WILL COME TO MY SIDE AND TOGETHER, WE WILL DEFEAT YOU!

FOR CANDACE, OUR NEIGHBORHOOD, AND ALL THE GOOD GELATIN LEFT IN THE WORLD!

MASTER?

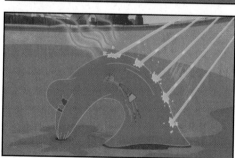

IT'S WORKING. HE'S MELTING DOWN THE DRAIN!

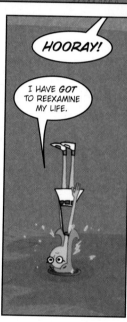

HOORAY!

I HAVE *GOT* TO REEXAMINE MY LIFE.

HERE THEY COME, PERRY THE PLATYPUS! HERE THEY COME, ALL OF MY MINIONS! *HA-HA-HA-HA!*

I COU-- I...

SOAP

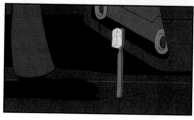

NOW YOU CAN *KOWTOW* BEFORE MY CARTILAGINOUS CREATION. IT'S SO **CORRUPT** AND **CANTANKEROUS** AND **CARNIVOROUS** AND, UH...

...UH, LOW IN **CALORIES** AND CA--CA...COW. COUCH. HM...AH, THAT'S ALL I GOT.

PERRY HAS A PLAN-- AND TAKES EXPERT AIM...

clink!

SP**OOOSH**!!

bzzt

bzzt

bzzt

KA**BOOM**!

MY *TURN-EVERYTHING-EVIL-INATOR!* **NO!**

RAARG!

16

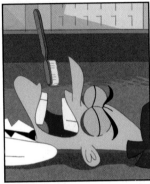

AND SO...

THE END!

"ELEMENTARY, MY DEAR STACY!"

SO KIDS, ARE YOU ENJOYING YOUR VISIT TO ENGLAND?

THERE'S NOTHING TO DO, GRANDMA.

WHAT? WHY DON'T YOU READ MY OLD *SHERLOCK HOLMES* BOOKS? I'VE GOT THE WHOLE COLLECTION RIGHT HERE.

GEE, THANKS MRS. FLETCHER.

DINNER'S AT 1900. THAT'S 7:00 FOR YOU YANKS.

AH, YES, READING. THAT'S WHAT THEY DID BEFORE THEY INVENTED *FUN*.

I HEARD THAT.

WELL, IT'S BETTER THAN NOTHING. MM? MMHMM. HMM...

THE NEXT MORNING...

OKAY, IS EVERYBODY READY?

WE'RE GOING TO TAKE YOU KIDS TO SEE THE *LONDON EYE.* IT'S ONE OF THE *LARGEST* FERRIS WHEELS IN THE ENTIRE *UNIVERSE.*

COOL.

GIRLS, ARE YOU READY?

WAI--WAI-- ALMOST FINISHED.

CANDACE, YOU STAYED UP ALL NIGHT JUST TO FINISH THAT *BOOK?*

NO, NO. WE FINISHED THE WHOLE *COLLECTION.*

HEY, WHERE'S PERRY?

OH, THERE HE IS.

SEE YOU LATER, OLD BOY. BE GOOD NOW.

GOOD MORNING, AGENT P.

DOOFENSHMIRTZ IS UP TO NO GOOD HERE IN THE U.K.*

*U.K.--UNITED KINGDOM!

AND, UH, AFTER YOUR *LAST* MISSION IN LONDON, WE RAN INTO SOME *TROUBLE* WITH THE BRITISH SPY UNION.

SO JOINING YOU TODAY IS *AGENT DOUBLE O-O,* AND JOINING *ME* TODAY IS THE LOVELY INSPECTOR INITIALS.

DOUBLE O-O, YOU AND AGENT P WILL BE ASSIGNED THE SAME MISSION AGAINST DR. DOOFENSHMIRTZ.

YOU REALIZE THIS MAN IS A PLATYPUS?

THEY'RE AMERICAN, DOUBLE O-O. JUST BE GLAD IT'S A *MAMMAL.*

WELL, GO GET HIM, AGENT P.

WHAT? THAT'S IT? NO FILES? NO LOCATION? NO CONTACT? WHAT KIND OF A MISSION *IS* THIS?

HMMPH! IT WAS ENOUGH FOR THE MAMMAL.

HEY, WHERE'S PHINEAS?

HERE ARE YOUR TICKETS FOR THE LONDON EYE.

DAD AND GRANDPA ARE GOING TO THE INTERNATIONAL HAGGIS FESTIVAL. WE'LL PICK YOU UP AROUND 4:15. BYE, KIDS.

HAVE FUN.

BYE.

CANDACE, YOU KNOW WHAT? FERB AND I WILL MEET YOU BACK HERE LATER. SEE YA!

BYE, GUYS!

DID YOU HEAR THAT? EVEN IN *ENGLAND*, MY BROTHERS HAVE SOME *SCHEME* PLANNED.

HOW CAN YOU TELL?

YOU DON'T HAVE TO BE SHERLOCK HOLMES TO--

OOH, STACY, THAT'S *IT!* WHO DID WE STAY UP ALL NIGHT LEARNING ABOUT? WHO IS THE *TOTAL KING* OF BUSTING?

SHERLOCK HOLMES?

YES. MAYBE I CAN FINALLY BUST THE BOYS ONCE AND FOR ALL IF I USE HOLMES' METHOD OF DEDUCTION!

COME ON, THIS WILL BE FUN! YOU COULD BE DR. WATSON!

ELSEWHERE...

THAT'S IT.

WE'RE TAKING *MY* CAR.

BY USING HOLMESY DEDUCTION, WE'LL BE ONE STEP AHEAD OF THE BOYS.

WE CAN GET MOM AND FINALLY SHOW HER--

AUTO SPARES

SPARES SERVICE

OOH! THERE THEY ARE.

NOW, WHY ARE THEY GOING INTO AN AUTO-PARTS STORE?

ALL RIGHT, WATSON. HERE'S WHERE THE DEDUCING BEGINS. THEY'VE...ACQUIRED A FLEET OF AUTOMOBILES, AND THEY'RE IN THERE BUYING A BUNCH OF LITTLE AIR FRESHENERS FOR THEM...OR... THEY'RE BUYING MOTOR OIL FOR THEIR *GIANT ROBOT!* WHAT DO YOU THINK, STACE?

STACE?

WHAT?

MEANWHILE, BENEATH BIG BEN...

knock knock

PERRY THE PLATYPUS!

OH, WHO'S YOUR LITTLE FRIEND HERE?

I'M AGENT DOUBLE O-O, FROM HER MAJESTY'S SECRET SERVICE.

DOUBLE O-O? ISN'T THAT JUST *TRIPLE O?*

NO, THAT'S *NOT* HOW YOU SAY IT.

IT SPELLS "OOO" DOESN'T IT?

IT'S JUST *DOUBLE O-O.*

HE'S *P* AND YOU'RE *OOO.* SO TOGETHER YOU SPELL...

NO, THEY'RE NOT "O'S," THEY'RE *ZEROS.* ALL RIGHT?

I WAS JUST GOING TO SAY "OOOP." LOOKS LIKE I STRUCK A NERVE THERE. *ANYWAY,* SHALL WE MOVE ON?

click!

I MUST APOLOGIZE. ALL OF MY TRAPS ARE PLATYPUS-SIZED.

CLAMP!

CLAMP!

WHAT ABOUT **THIS** THEN?

OH, THAT.

YOU SEE, AS I GET OLDER, I FIND IT'S HARDER AND HARDER TO READ MY SMALL, LITTLE WRISTWATCH.

SO I WILL LAUNCH BIG BEN INTO SPACE...

WHEEEE!

...AND FLY IT ALL THE WAY TO THE TRI-STATE AREA.

LA, LA, LA. HERE I AM. LA, LA, LA.

I JUST WOKE UP, AND I WANT TO KNOW WHAT TIME IT IS.

YES, I AM A **GENIUS!**

SO THAT... THAT'S YOUR WHOLE PLAN?

WELL, IN A NUTSHELL, YES. WHAT DO YOU THINK?

AM I ON ONE OF THOSE HIDDEN-CAMERA SHOWS?

YOU REALIZE YOU COULD JUST **BUY** A BIGGER WATCH. OR MAYBE A **WALL CLOCK?**

YES, BUT THEN I WOULD HAVE TO DRIVE TO A **STORE** AND FIND A **PARKING SPACE.** THEN YOU HAVE TO CHOOSE FROM, LIKE, **DOZENS** OF STYLES.

IT JUST SEEMED LIKE SO MUCH **WORK.** THIS WILL BE MUCH LESS COMPLICATED.

BACK TO SHERLOCK AND WATSON...

EXCUSE ME, SIR. WERE THESE TWO BOYS IN HERE EARLIER?

WELL, THEM TWO THINGS WERE HANGIN' ABOUT, AND THEY HAD A BIT OF A BUTCHERS, AND, UH, WHIRLS AROUND THE BACK AND CARTED OFF SOME OLD BANGERS THAT I DIDN'T NEED.

OY, AREN'T THEY A BIT HAIRLESS FOR THEM KINDA BUSHIES?

UH... STACY?

I'M WORKING ON IT. AH. HE SAID, "THEY WERE HERE. THEY CARTED AWAY SOME JUNK FROM OUT BACK." AND, "AREN'T THEY A LITTLE YOUNG TO BE DOING THAT?"

YES. YES, THEY ARE.

AHA. IT'S CRAWLING WITH CLUES OUT HERE.

HMM, LOOK AT THESE CIRCULAR INDENTATIONS IN THE DIRT. AND THE SUBTLE SCENT OF RUBBER IN THE AIR. BY JOVE, STACY, *WHAT COULD IT BE?*

UH, FREE TIRES?

FREE TIRES

MAYBE, MAYBE. WE NEED MORE CLUES.

FIRST CLUE--TIRES. SECOND CLUE-- PINEAPPLE.

THIRD CLUE-- BUTTER.

FOURTH CLUE-- PIPES.

STACY, I THINK I'M CLOSE TO FIGURING IT OUT!

MEANWHILE...

CLUNK!

PSSHHH... RUMBLE RUMBLE

WELL, I'M GOING UP TO THE TOP OF THE TOWER.

I'M SURE YOU TWO WILL HAVE A *HOT TIME* TOGETHER. *HA-HA-HA-HA!*

DON'T WORRY, AGENT P.

I'LL HAVE US OUT OF THESE BEFORE YOU KNOW IT.

UNDERNEATH BIG BEN...

JUST A FEW MORE MINUTES.

beep!

CLANK!

YOWCH!

OH, THERE YOU GO. GOOD THING I HAD THE WATCH-LASER.

DOOFENSHMIRTZ TOOK THE STAIRS...

...BUT IF WE WORK OUR WAY UP THROUGH THE INNER MECHANISMS OF THE CLOCK, HE'LL NEVER SEE US COMING.

HUP!

HUP!

HUP!

HUP!

ding!

AT STREET LEVEL...

WHOA! CANDACE, YOU'RE AMAZING, YOU TOTALLY FIGURED IT OUT!

YEAH, I GUESS I DID. NOW, ON TO THE BUSTING.

WHEE!

NEXT!

WOO-HOO!

PHINEAS!

I FIGURED YOU GUYS WERE UP TO SOMETHING.

OH, HEY, GUYS! DO YOU LIKE IT?

THE TIRES, THE PIPES. I SEE WHAT THOSE WERE FOR...

...BUT WHAT WAS WITH THE PINEAPPLE?

OH, THAT WAS FOR FERB. HE WAS HUNGRY.

OH, AND THE BUTTER, TOO, HUH?

NO, NO.

HE'S USING THAT FOR SPEED.

IT'S A NEW WORLD RECORD!

MOM'S GONNA *FLIP* WHEN SHE HEARS ABOUT THIS.

CLAMP!

HELLO?

GARBBIBLGLUBBLEGURGLEBLARG!

SOMEONE WITH A THICK COCKNEY ACCENT. WRONG NUMBER.

WAAAAAHH!!

AIEEEE!!!

CAN I TAKE A TURN?

GO FOR IT.

WHEE!

THAT'S WHAT I'M TALKING ABOUT!

STACY! OOH! IT'S 4:15. MOM SHOULD BE HERE.

WELL, IT'S ABOUT TIME.

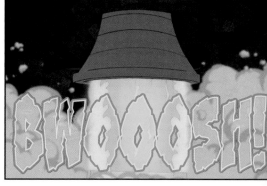

BWOOOSH!

UH, CANDACE?

NOT NOW, STACY, THERE'S MOM! *MOM! MOM!*

MOM, YOU'VE GOTTA--

OH, YES, LOOK AT YOUR CUTE OUTFIT.

NO, MOM, YOU GOTTA LOOK AT--

OH, BIG BEN. GORGEOUS.

BUT, BUT, BUT BUT, BUT--

AH, HERE COME THE BOYS.

HEY, MOM! YOU MISSED ALL THE FUN.

LOOKS LIKE WE DID. ALL RIGHT, LET'S CATCH A CAB AND HEAD HOME. COME ON.

LOOKS LIKE CANDACE AND STACY DID SOME SHOPPING.

I'LL NEVER UNDERSTAND FASHION.

THE END!

The Chronicles of MEAP

MEAP!

ADAPTED BY JOHN GREEN

BASED ON THE SERIES CREATED BY
DAN POVENMIRE & JEFF "SWAMPY" MARSH

DISNEY PRESS
NEW YORK

LIBRARY OF CONGRESS CATALOG CARD NUMBER ON FILE.
ISBN 978-1-4231-4055-9
FIRST EDITION
1 3 5 7 9 10 8 6 4 2
PRINTED IN THE UNITED STATES OF AMERICA
G658-7729-4-10152

FOR MORE DISNEY PRESS FUN, VISIT WWW.DISNEYBOOKS.COM
VISIT DISNEYCHANNEL.COM

The Chronicles of MEAP

IT'S THE BOTTOM OF THE NINTH INNING. BASES ARE LOADED. IT ALL COMES DOWN TO THIS FINAL PITCH FROM FERB "THE CURVE" FLETCHER.

HERE'S THE WINDUP...

POOMF!

AND IT'S A STEEERIII--

veep veep

--IIIII--

--IIIKE! AND THE CROWD GOES WILD!

THERE'S THE LESSON, BASEBALL FANS--NEVER JUDGE A BOOK BY ITS COVER.

MEANWHILE, INSIDE...

BORING, DULL, STUPID, LAME, HEAVY-HANDED, AND DERIVATIVE.

OH, THANK YOU FOR THOSE INSIGHTFUL REVIEWS OF *BOOKS* YOU HAVEN'T READ.

MOM, THAT'S WHY BOOKS HAVE COVERS-- TO *JUDGE* THEM. I MEAN, WHY DID YOU CHOOSE *THESE* BOOKS FROM THE LIBRARY?

THEY...LOOKED INTERESTING...

SO...

POINT TAKEN.

OKAY, HONEY, I'M OFF TO HELP DAD AT THE ANTIQUE STORE.

OOH, HEY, HERE'S A PACKAGE FOR YOU!

MY BANGO-RU!

YOUR WHAT?

MY BANGO-RU! THEY'RE THESE ADORABLE JAPANESE CHARACTERS THAT ARE SO *IN* RIGHT NOW. LIKE, IN A KITSCHY WAY.

THE GUITARIST FOR THE BETTYS HAS ONE PAINTED ON HER GUITAR! STACY AND I DESIGNED OUR OWN DOLLS ONLINE.

WELL, ASSUMING NONE OF THAT IS TEENAGE CODE FOR SOMETHING I SHOULD BE WORRIED ABOUT AS A PARENT, I'M OFF.

BYE, MOM! I'M GONNA CALL STACY!

BANGO-RU!

BANGO-RU! I JUST GOT MY LITTLE BUNNY-BEAR! IT'S A CROSS BETWEEN A BUNNY AND A BEAR. YA GET IT?

IT'S THE MOST PRECIOUS THING.

I JUST GOT MINE TOO! HE'S A CROSS BETWEEN A COW AND A FROG. I'M CALLING HIM SEÑOR FROWG. HE'S GONNA BE THE CUTEST THING! YOU'RE JUST GONNA--

Bango-Ru!

AAAIIEEEE!!!

CANDACE? WHAT'S GOING ON?

I JUST DISCOVERED WHY COWS AND FROGS DON'T DATE.

WELL, WE'LL STILL HAVE FUN AT THE BANGO-RU CONVENTION TODAY.

YEAH, I GUESS.

OKAY, FERB, LET'S SEE WHAT THIS BAD BOY CAN DO! GO LONG!

POP FLY!

COOL!

CRACK!

OH, HERE IT COMES.

UM, HEY, FERB? I KNOW WHAT WE'RE GONNA DO TODAY-- *RUN FOR OUR LIVES!*

KERSHPOOM!

WHOA, I THINK WE MAY HAVE JUST STOPPED AND/OR STARTED AN ALIEN INVASION.

pssh...

I HOPE HE'S NOT TOO ANGRY...OR HUNGRY.

MEAP.

WOW, THAT IS *CUTE.* HEY, ARE YOU OKAY? WE'RE REALLY SORRY ABOUT YOUR SHIP.

MEAP.

WHAT'S YOUR NAME?

MEAP.

HI, MEAP! I'M PHINEAS, AND THIS IS FERB.

MEAP.

WHAT YOU GOT THERE? HEY, THIS MUST BE HIS FATHER.

DON'T WORRY, MEAP. WE'LL FIX YOUR SHIP, AND YOU'LL BE WITH YOUR DAD IN NO TIME!

"HEY, FERB, I KNOW WHAT WE'RE GONNA DO TODAY! LET'S GET OURSELVES TOTALLY BUSTED BY CRASHING OUR STUPID TOY IN THE BACKYARD!"

OH, HI, CANDACE! IT ISN'T A TOY. IT'S A REAL, LIVE ALIEN SPACESHIP!

OH, GOOD, BECAUSE THIS ISN'T A CELL PHONE. IT'S AN INTERGALACTIC LITTLE-BROTHER BUSTERIZER, WHICH I'LL USE ON YOU IF YOU DON'T CLEAN UP THIS MESS!

HUH?

OH, THAT IS THE MOST **ADORABLE** THING I'VE EVER SEEN IN MY LIFE. YOU GUYS MADE A BANGO-RU DOLL?

MEAP.

HE **TALKS?**

WELL, MORE THAN FERB, BUT "MEAP" IS PRETTY MUCH THE ONLY THING HE SAYS.

WELL, YOU AND YOUR LITTLE **BANGO-ROBOT** BETTER NOT SHOW UP AT THE CONVENTION AND MAKE ME LOOK BAD!

MEAP.

OKAY! LET'S FIX US AN ALIEN SPACESHIP!

HEY, FERB, HAVE YOU SEEN PERRY?

SPEAKING OF PERRY...

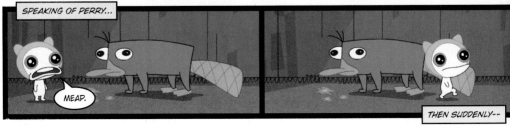

MEAP.

THEN SUDDENLY--

8

CHANGE!

GOOD MORNING, AGENT P! I WONDER WHAT EXCITING MISSION WE HAVE FOR YOU TODAY... *DOOFENSHMIRTZ* HAS PURCHASED A LOT OF *CARPET.*

HE MUST BE UP TO SOMETHING BAD, BECAUSE HE'S A BAD, *BAD* MAN.

HE'S *THIS* BAD! HA-HA-HA...

I CAN'T KEEP THIS UP. CARL WAS DOING MY ARMS, SEE?

OH, TOO FUNNY.

ANYWAYS, STOP DOOFENSHMIRTZ WITH THE CARPET THING.

BACK IN THE YARD...

HI, GUYS. WHAT'CHA DOIN'?

OH, HI, ISABELLA! WE'RE FIXING UP THIS SPACESHIP THAT BELONGS TO OUR NEW FRIEND, MEAP.

HEH, HEH. MEAP.

HE'S THE MOST ADORABLE THING IN THE WORLD.

REALLY? ARE YOU SURE THERE'S NOTHING OR NO ONE THAT'S *MORE* ADORABLE?

NO. NOT A CHANCE.

HERE, SEE FOR YOURSELF. MEAP? *MEAP?*

BANGO-RU!

BANGO-RU.

OH, CANDACE! YOUR BANGO-RU! IT'S SO CUTE, I COULD *DIE!*

WHAT? OH, NO--

MEAP.

AND IT MAKES LITTLE NOISES! HOW DID YOU DO THAT?

OH, WELL, PHINEAS AND FERB, YOU KNOW?

OH, THEY TRICKED IT OUT FOR YOU. *COOL*. COME ON! LET'S GO TO THE CONVENTION.

RIGHT BEHIND YOU!

YOUR REIGN OF TERROR HAS COME TO AN END, SEÑOR FROWG!

OKAY, I RIGGED FERB'S OLD GPS DEVICE TO CREATE A *CUTE TRACKER.* IT LOCKS ONTO THE CUTEST THING IN THE AREA, SO IT *SHOULD* LEAD US RIGHT TO MEAP! *OOH,* I GOT SOMETHING!

OH, THAT'S PROBABLY ME. SORRY.

NO. IT'S THREE MILES IN *THAT* DIRECTION. WANNA COME AND HELP ME FIND MEAP?

SURE! I STILL HAVE TO GET MY YOU-WOULDN'T-KNOW-CUTE-IF-IT-BIT-YOUR-LEGS-OFF ACCOMPLISHMENT PATCH!

COOL! LET'S GO!

MEANWHILE, DOOFENSHMIRTZ EVIL, INC. IS CARPETED!

BLAST!

AH, PERRY THE PLATYPUS!

JUST IN TIME FOR YOUR LITTLE LESSON IN *STATIC ELECTRICITY!*

beep!

GRAB!

rub rub rub

FOOMP!

HA! IT LOOKS LIKE I RUBBED YOU THE WRONG WAY, *PUFFY THE FUZZYPUS!*

YOU MIGHT ASK--WHY THE CARPET? WHAT IS HE DOING? WHAT'S GOING ON? WHY IS HE LISTING QUESTIONS I MIGHT ASK HIM?

WELL, I BELIEVE THE ANSWERS ARE BEST EXPRESSED IN BACKSTORY FORM...

WHEN I WAS A BOY, I GOT A BALLOON AT A CARNIVAL. I DREW A FACE ON HIM. I SPRAYED HIM WITH A SPECIAL *LIFELONG* LASTING SPRAY I CREATED. AND I NAMED HIM *"BALLOONY."*

HE BECAME MY BEST FRIEND IN THE WHOLE WORLD... *YADA, YADA, YADA...* THEN ONE TRAGIC DAY WHEN I WAS PROTECTING OUR GARDEN AS A LAWN GNOME--

HE'S STILL OUT THERE SOMEWHERE. NOT TO PUT TOO FINE A POINT ON IT, BUT I PUT THAT *LONG-LASTING SPRAY* ON HIM, SO HE'S STILL AROUND!

--WHATEVER, YOU REMEMBER *THAT* BACKSTORY-- BALLOONY STARTED FLOATING AWAY. I TRIED TO REACH OUT AND GRAB HIM, BUT I NEVER SAW BALLOONY AGAIN.

AND I PLAN TO BRING HIM TO ME.

BALLOONS, YOU SEE, ARE DRAWN TO STATIC ELECTRICITY, SO I CREATED *THIS!*

BEHOLD THE STATIC-ELECTRO AMPLIFINATOR!

BUP, BUP, BUP, KEEP-KEEP BEHOLDING... KEEP BEHOLDING...BEHOLDING... AND WE'RE STILL BEHOLDING... AAAAND SCENE.

ELSEWHERE...

beep!

FWOOM!

MEANWHILE, NOT THAT DEEP IN SPACE...

WHAT'S THIS?

WARP-DRIVE SIGNATURE DETECTED.

HA-HA! I HAVE YOU NOW.

ELSEWHERE...

BANGO-RU!

THIS IS *SO* WEIRD.

IT'S LIKE A STRANGE ALIEN WORLD.

OOH, BANGO-RU PURSES! HOW *CUTE!*

I THINK I SAW THAT ONE ON THE RED CARPET THE OTHER NIGHT!

HEY! IS THIS *YOUR* DOLL, YOUNG LADY? I FOUND IT ABANDONED ON THE FLOOR OVER THERE. YOUR *IRRESPONSIBILITY* MAKES *MY* JOB AS SECURITY GUARD A MILLION TIMES HARDER!

WHA--? IRRESPONSIBLE KIDS!

I COULD HAVE TRIPPED OVER IT! YOU COULD HAVE KILLED ME! I'M LUCKY TO BE ALIVE!

YOU'RE IN *BIG* TROUBLE--

THE CUTE SIGNAL'S GETTING STRONGER. ALTHOUGH I KEEP GETTING THIS WEIRD CUTE INTERFERENCE FROM SOMEWHERE.

IT'S ME! I'M ENDANGERING THE MISSION. I SHOULDN'T HAVE COME.

NO, IT'S MEAP'S SPACESHIP! WHOA, **SWEET!** YOU TRICKED IT OUT, FERB! ISABELLA AND I ARE HOT ON MEAP'S TRAIL. LET'S BOUNCE!

THEY CAN'T BAN ME FROM **BANGO-RU** CONVENTIONS FOR LIFE!

I BAN MYSELF!

AND WHAT KIND OF TOY **ARE** YOU, ANYWAY?

HEY, CANDACE, YOU FOUND MEAP!

UH, MORE LIKE HE FOUND ME...?

WELL, HIS SHIP'S FIXED, SO HE CAN GET BACK TO HIS FAMILY NOW!

ZAP!

WHAT'S HAPPENING?

GOTCHA!

WE'RE CAUGHT IN SOME KIND OF TRACTOR BEAM.

IT'S PULLING US IN! MAYBE IT'S THE SPACE AUTHORITIES. DID WE DO SOMETHING WRONG?

WELL, IT OCCURS TO ME THAT PERHAPS NOT *ALL* OF THE MODIFICATIONS I MADE ARE TECHNICALLY "STREET LEGAL."

WHAT'S GOING ON? *WAIT! COME BACK!* WHO WAS THAT?

THAT WAS YOUR FATHER?

MEAP.

OH, IT'S *NOT* YOUR FATHER? IT'S A MUG SHOT?

OH, NO! PHINEAS AND FERB HAVE BEEN ABDUCTED BY AN INTERGALACTIC CRIMINAL!

MEAP.

WHERE'S HE TAKING US?

LOOK, HE'S HEADED FOR THAT SMALL CLOUD.

THAT'S NO CLOUD. THAT'S A **SPACE STATION.**

I'VE GOT A GOOD FEELING ABOUT THIS!

VrrrrrM...

HA! YOU THOUGHT YOU WERE CLEVER DISGUISING YOUR SHIP, BUT I GOT YOU NOW...! WHOEVER...YOU... ARE...

HEY, LOOK, IT'S MEAP'S DAD!

ALL RIGHT, WHAT THE **HECK** IS GOING ON?! IS THIS SOME KIND OF **JOKE?**

I'M PHINEAS. THAT'S ISABELLA, AND THIS IS FERB.

WHAT'S **YOUR** NAME?

I AM KNOWN BY MANY NAMES THROUGHOUT THE UNIVERSE. WELL, **TWO** MAINLY--"MITCH" AND, UH, SOME OF THE GUYS CALL ME "BIG MITCH."

ANYWAY, WHERE'D YOU GET THIS SHIP?

IT'S MEAP'S SHIP... AND DON'T WORRY, HE'S JUST FINE.

OH, GOOD, GOOD...AND EXACTLY WHO IS "MEAP"?

WELL, THAT'S WHAT **WE** CALL HIM 'CAUSE IT'S ALL HE SAYS.

MEAP? ABOUT YEA HIGH, BIG EYES?

THE BIGGEST!

KINDA LOOKS LIKE THIS?

UPCOMING EVENTS

THAT'S MEAP!

THAT'S MY *MORTAL ENEMY!*

REALLY? HE SEEMS LIKE SUCH A NICE GUY.

HE IS! *I'M* NOT!

YOU SEE, I STEAL RARE CREATURES FROM THEIR HOME WORLDS AND IMPRISON THEM HERE ON MY SHIP. I'M A--

YOU'RE A *POACHER!* THAT'S *WRONG.* THESE POOR CREATURES SHOULDN'T BE LOCKED UP HERE! THEY SHOULD BE BROUGHT BACK TO THEIR HOMES AND SET FREE!

OH, *REALLY?* MAYBE I SHOULD LOCK YOU THREE UP IN HERE AS WELL.

NAH, THAT'S COOL. TONIGHT'S TACO NIGHT AT HOME!

MEANWHILE...

HI, MOM. PHINEAS AND FERB HAVE BEEN ABDUCTED BY AN EVIL ALIEN, AND I'M HERE WITH ANOTHER ALIEN WHO ISN'T HIS SON, AND--

HOW DOES THAT SOUND SO FAR?

I AGREE. CRAY-ZEE!

WHAT ARE WE GONNA DO?

PLAY CATCH?

HMM. WELL, IF YOU THINK IT'LL HELP.

PHINEAS AND FERB.

YOUR FATHER.

NO, RIGHT, NOT YOUR FATHER. A BAD GUY.

THEY'RE IN A GIANT SPACESHIP.

BUT HOW ARE WE SUPPOSED TO GET UP THERE AND SAVE THEM?

veep veep

OH, I GET IT!

DUH! YOU'RE TRYING TO TELL ME SOMETHING!

WHAT?

SO YOU KNOW WHEN YOU WALK AROUND IN SOCKS AND RUB THEM ON THE CARPET, YOU GET THAT LITTLE STATIC SHOCK?

BEHOLD THE NEW UNIFORM OF *PURE EVIL!* I CALL IT THE *SOCKY SHOCKY SUITY.*

ON SECOND THOUGHT...

OH, COOL! CHECK THESE CREATURES OUT!

WOULD YOU THREE SIT STILL? YOU DON'T GET IT. YOU'RE MY *PRISONERS!*

YOU SHOULD BE *AFRAID* OF ME!

AH, LIKE A MOTH TO THE FLAME.

YOU KIDS MIGHT BE OF SOME USE TO ME AF-- *HEY!* DON'T GO IN THERE! YOU'LL TRACK DIRT BACK INTO THE CORRIDOR!

ARGH! I'LL DEAL WITH THEM LATER!

WHOA! I'VE GOT THIS SITUATION –:GULP:– TOTALLY UNDER CONTROL.

LOOK AT THE SIZE OF THAT THING!

WOW. CHECK *THIS* PLACE OUT.

I KNOW HOW TO FIND PHINEAS AND FERB. THEY'LL BE WHERE THE *COOL* STUFF IS.

OKAY, I'LL GO IN AND GET THEM. YOU STAY HERE. THIS COULD GET *DANGEROUS.*

22

SO WE MEET AGAIN.

MEAP.

I AGREE. IT ENDS *HERE*.

OH, AND BY THE WAY, I TALKED TO YOUR LITTLE FRIENDS, AND JUST SO WE'RE CLEAR, I AM *NOT* YOUR FATHER!

OKAY, I'M ALMOST DONE CHARGING UP THE SOCKY SHOCKY SUITY SUIT.

zwip *zwip*

YOU KNOW, IT'S THE TECHNICAL SIDE OF EVIL THAT I THINK PEOPLE DON'T REALLY APPRECIATE.

zwip

THERE! NOW WATCH AS EVERY BALLOON IN THE ENTIRE TRI-STATE AREA IS RIPPED FROM THE HANDS OF CHILDREN AND CLOWNS AND CLOWN CHILDREN!

CHARGE!

ARGH!

24

WOW. THAT'S A LOT OF BALLOONS!

WHAAA--!

YOU KNOW, ON *PAPER*...

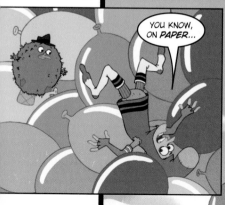

...-*SIGH*- THIS WAS THE OUTCOME TOO.

SUDDENLY-- MEAP! OH, YEAH? WELL-- CRUNCH!

OH, MAN, WHAT THE--?

WE'RE RIGHT IN THE MIDDLE OF A SHOWDOWN, IF YOU DON'T MIND.

OH, OH, *I* GET IT. NEMESIS CONFRONTATION, EH? IT LOOKS SERIOUS. ONE OF THOSE "IT ENDS HERE" KIND OF THINGS...

HEH-HEH. NOT FUN.

WELL, DON'T MIND ME. I'M JUST "PLAYING" THROUGH, AS THEY SAY. I'LL SHOW MYSELF OUT.

beep!

NO, THAT'S WHERE I KEEP--

IT'S *YOU!*

BALLOONY!

HEY, THAT'S THE MOST UNIQUE CREATURE IN MY COLLECTION-- *COLIN,* MY BEST FRIEND.

WHAT? THAT'S BALLOONY, *MY* BEST FRIEND!

NO, I-I FOUND COLIN JUST FLOATING ALL ALONE IN SPACE.

WELL, *I* ACTUALLY DREW HIS FACE! LOOK, LOOK, I SIGNED IT!

Heinz

COLIN. *FEH!* COME ON, BALLOONY. LET'S SCOOT.

B-BALLOONY?

HA! SEE? COLIN IS *MY* BEST FRIEND!

YOU'VE *CHANGED,* BALLOONY! AND I THOUGHT YOU WERE ACTUALLY BACKSTORY-WORTHY! IT MAKES ME *SICK!*

WELL, I DON'T EVEN NEED YOU ANYMORE! YEAH, I'VE GOT AN EVEN *BETTER* BEST FRIEND!

HE'S A REALLY GOOD LISTENER. HE EVEN PUT UP WITH ME GOING ON ABOUT HOW GREAT YOU WERE. *HA!*

IT'S CLEAR TO ME NOW THAT MY *REAL* BEST FRIEND IS PERRY THE PLAT--

PUNCH!

AAAAIIEEE!!

UH, HELLO? FALLING TO MY DOOM HERE!

OH, *HI,* PERRY THE PLATYPUS! SEE? MY BEST FRIEND WILL SAVE ME...YOU ARE SAVING ME, RIGHT?

NOW THAT *THAT'S* OVER WITH...

beep!

SLAM!

ALL TOO EASY.

27

THAT WAS *AWESOME!*

I KNEW THERE WAS STILL MORE COOL STUFF TO DO IN SPACE!

UH-OH.

BOOM!

BOOM!

BOOM!

STRIKE THREE. THEY'RE OUT!

COOL! THANKS, CANDACE!

HEY, WHERE'S MEAP? I TOLD HIM TO WAIT RIGHT HERE.

I'LL TRY TO FIND HIM ON MY CUTE METER, BUT I'VE BEEN HAVING TROUBLE PICKING UP HIS CUTE SIGNAL.

PHINEAS, SINCE YOU OBVIOUSLY WON'T FIGURE THIS OUT ON YOUR OWN, I THINK *I'M* THE ONE CAUSING THE CUTE INTERFERENCE.

DON'T BE SILLY, ISABELLA.

I TOOK INTO ACCOUNT YOUR CUTENESS AND ADJUSTED THE SETTINGS FROM THE BEGINNING! SEE, LOOK WHAT HAPPENS IF I CHANGE IT BACK TO NORMAL...

OOPS. SO MUCH FOR FINDING MEAP.

DO YOU THINK HE'S OKAY?

NO. NO, I DON'T.

FOOLISH CHILDREN. ONLY NOW DO YOU UNDERSTAND YOUR GRAVE SITUATION.

MEAP!

HI, MITCH!

"HI, MITCH! LOOK AT THE COOL STUFF, MITCH! BLAH, BLAH, BLAH, MITCH!"

I MEAN, SERIOUSLY? SERIOUSLY? YOU'RE *STILL* NOT GETTING THIS? YOU'RE ALL TRAPPED ON MY SHIP FOREVER, LIKE ANIMALS IN A CAGE! *GET IT?* YOU *LOST!* I *WON!*

veep!

BONK!

HI, MITCH!

MEAP.

HUH?

WHAM!

OOF!

I--I DON'T BELIEVE IT.

O-O-OKAY, OKAY, I *SURRENDER!*

YOU--YOU CAN STOP BEHAVING IN A WAY COUNTERINTUITIVE TO HOW YOU SUPERFICIALLY APPEAR! WE *GET* IT!

HEY, STAY AWAY FROM MY *UNIVERSAL MUSTACHE TRANSLATOR!*

RIIIPP!

OW!

MEAP!

CHILDREN, *THANK YOU* FOR YOUR HELP IN BRINGING DOWN THIS *VILLAINOUS SCOUNDREL.*

YOU SEE, I AM AN *INTERGALACTIC SECURITY AGENT* WHO ROAMS THE UNIVERSE...

...*BUSTING* PEOPLE WHO DO STUFF THEY'RE NOT SUPPOSED TO DO.

YOU'RE LIKE THE *ME* OF THE GALAXY!

EXACTLY. I AM PLEASED TO HAVE NOT ONLY MADE SOME TRUE FRIENDS, BUT TO HAVE MET A KINDRED SPIRIT AS WELL.

I THOUGHT MEAP WAS A HELPLESS LITTLE CREATURE.

HUH. I GUESS I LEARNED TO NEVER JUDGE A BOOK BY ITS COVER AGAIN!

BLARG BLARG GURGLE BLARG!

AAAAAHH!! AN ALIEN MONSTER! GET TO THE SHIP!

UM, ACTUALLY, THAT'S MY MOTHER-IN-LAW, SO...HEH-HEH...YEAH, SHE'S CORRECT.

LET'S GET OUTTA HERE!

NEXT TIME ON THE CHRONICLES OF MEAP...

MEAP.

...MEAPLESS IN SEATTLE!

THE EN[